The Colony of North Carolina

A Primary Source History

The Rosen Publishing Group's

PowerKids Press™

PRIMARY SOURCE

Melody S. Mis

To Debbi, Gene, and Toni Murray

Published in 2007 by The Rosen Publishing Group, Inc.
29 East 21st Street, New York, NY 10010

First Edition

Editor: Jennifer Way
Book Design: Ginny Chu
Layout Design: Julio Gil
Photo Researcher: Amy Feinberg

Photo Credits: Cover, pp. 8, 12 © North Wind Picture Archives; p. 4 © The Mariners' Museum, p. 4 (inset) © Bettmann/Corbis; p. 6 Bildarchiv Preussischer Kulturbesitz/Art Resource, NY; pp. 6 (inset), 8 (inset), 10 North Carolina State Archives; p. 10 (inset) Library of Congress/Bridgeman Art Library; p. 12 (inset) © Sotheby's/akg-images; p. 14 © Getty Images; p. 14 (inset) New Hanover County Public Library; p. 16 Private Collection, © Royal Exchange Art Gallery at Cork Street, London/ Bridgeman Art Library; p. 16 (inset) © Chris Aydlett, for the Cupola House; p. 18 The Free Library of Philadelphia; p. 18 (inset) Rare Books and Special Collections Division, Library of Congress; p. 20 National Park Service, Harpers Ferry Center, artist Gil Cohen; p. 20 (inset) The New York Public Library/Art Resource, NY.

Library of Congress Cataloging-in-Publication Data

Mis, Melody S.
   The colony of North Carolina : a primary source history / Melody S. Mis.— 1st ed.
      p. cm. — (The primary source library of the thirteen colonies and the Lost Colony)
   Includes index.
   ISBN 1-4042-3436-5 (library binding)
   1. North Carolina—History—Colonial period, ca. 1600–1775—Juvenile literature. 2. North Carolina—History—1775–1865—Juvenile literature. 3. North Carolina—History—Colonial period, ca. 1600–1775—Sources—Juvenile literature. 4. North Carolina—History—1775–1865—Sources—Juvenile literature. I. Title. II. Series.
   F257.M57 2007
   975.6'02—dc22
                                        2005026712

Manufactured in the United States of America

Contents

This 1590 map shows the coastline and the islands off the coast of today's North Carolina. Inset: Giovanni da Verrazano explored North Carolina's coast in the 1520s. He lived from 1485 to 1528.

Discovering North Carolina

North Carolina's first **inhabitants** were Native American groups, such as the Tuscarora, the Catawba, and the Cherokee. These Native Americans were living in North Carolina when the first Europeans landed there in the 1500s.

The first European to visit North Carolina was the Italian explorer Giovanni da Verrazano in 1524. He was looking for a trade route, or way, through North America to Asia. Although Verrazano did not find a route to Asia, he explored the North Carolina coastline. An English group settled on an island off the coast of North Carolina 60 years later.

In 1584, Elizabeth I, queen of England, granted land in North Carolina to Walter Raleigh. In 1587, Raleigh sent settlers there. They founded a colony on Roanoke Island. When supply ships came to Roanoke in 1590, the colonists were gone! No one knows what happened to the Roanoke settlement, which is known as the Lost Colony.

This picture shows a Quaker service, called a meeting. Inset: Charles II granted the 1663 charter for Carolina to eight proprietors. These men were Edward Hyde, the Earl of Clarendon, George Monck, the Duke of Albemarle, Lord William Craven, Lord John Berkley, Lord Anthony Ashley Cooper, Sir George Carteret, Sir William Berkley, and Sir John Colleton.

Founding the Eleventh Colony

In 1663, King Charles II gave the land that would become North Carolina and South Carolina to a group of eight men. These men were called **proprietors**. The proprietors were all important friends of the king's. They promised to use the land to establish a colony and to rent land to settlers.

Colonists from neighboring Virginia had settled in the northeast corner of North Carolina in the 1650s. After the proprietors got their land grant in 1663, they wanted more people from Virginia to settle in North Carolina. They told the newcomers that they would not have to pay taxes for one year and that they would have religious freedom. This led **Quakers** from England and Virginia to move to North Carolina. These people were being **persecuted** because they did not belong to the Church of England.

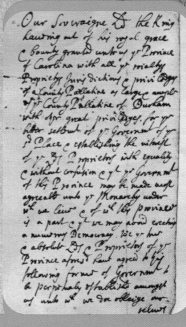

From Fundamental Constitutions of Carolina

"Our sovereign lord the King having, out of his royal grace and bounty, granted unto us the province of Carolina. . . . [w]e, the lords and proprietors of the province aforesaid, have agreed to this following form of government, to be perpetually established amongst us, unto which we do oblige ourselves, our heirs and successors, In the most binding ways that can be devised."

The opening part of the Fundamental Constitutions says that Carolina's proprietors have agreed to establish a government that will operate as a colony under the king of England.

North Carolina's early European settlers cut down trees to clear the land and used the wood to build homes. They planted corn, beans, rice, and wheat for food and also to trade with England. Inset: The 1669 Fundamental Constitutions of Carolina planned a government for the colony.

Settling North Carolina

Colonists from Virginia and Massachusetts began to settle in North Carolina around 1665. They cut down trees to clear the land for their farms. The proprietors established North Carolina's first government. They chose William Drummond to be the governor and granted the colonists an **elected assembly**.

In 1669, the proprietors raised the rent on the colonists' land. Many North Carolinians **protested** by refusing to pay the rent. In 1677, the colonists protested because Governor Thomas Miller was taxing them too much. They arrested Miller and put him in jail during what is called Culpeper's Rebellion.

In 1677, Thomas Miller became North Carolina's governor. Miller raised taxes and refused the vote to people he disliked. John Culpeper and a group of men threw Miller in Albemarle County's jail. When Miller escaped from jail and returned to England, Culpeper followed him. Both men told their story to the proprietors, who sided with Culpeper and sent a new governor to the colony.

Christoph von Graffenried made this sketch, which shows settlers and slaves being captured in the Tuscarora War. The war had broken out one year after he had led settlers from Germany and Switzerland to North Carolina. Inset: This picture of Blackbeard was taken from a book about famous pirates. Blackbeard regularly hid out on Okracoke Island in North Carolina.

North Carolina's Early Years

By the late 1600s, North Carolina and South Carolina each had its own governor, even though the colony would not be separated until 1712. In 1691, the proprietors put South Carolina's governor in charge of North Carolina. South Carolina's governor then hired an assistant governor from North Carolina.

North Carolina's first town, Bath, was founded in 1705. In 1710, John Lawson and Baron Christoph von Graffenried led settlers from Switzerland and Germany to found New Bern. It was the colony's capital until the **American Revolution**.

From 1711 to 1713, the North Carolinians fought the Tuscarora War. The Tuscarora were angry because colonists were taking their land. The **pirate** Blackbeard attacked North Carolina's ships during this period. The attacks ended after Blackbeard was killed in 1718.

This woodcut shows William Tryon talking to the Regulators during the Regulators' War. The Regulators felt that their interests were not represented in the Colonial government. Inset: George II was born in 1683 and died in 1760. This painting of him was made in 1738. In 1729, North Carolina became a royal colony under George II.

The Regulators' War

In 1729, North Carolina became a royal colony. This meant it was ruled by the king. During the next 30 years, the colony's population grew from 30,000 to about 110,000.

In 1768, the settlers in western North Carolina became angry, because they were not **represented** in the colony's government. Assemblymen from western North Carolina had trouble attending the assembly's meetings. This was because it was a long distance to the capital in New Bern. To protest their lack of representation, some westerners formed a group called the Regulators. When the Regulators attacked government workers, Governor William Tryon sent **minutemen** to find them. On May 16, 1771, the minutemen beat the Regulators during the battle at Almance Creek. This was part of what became known as the Regulators' War, which lasted from 1764 until 1771.

CONTINUATION OF

(November 20.) THE (Numb. 58.)

NORTH-CAROLINA GAZETTE.

WILMINGTON, November 20.

From the *North-Carolina Gazette*

" . . . [n]ear Five Hundred People assembled together in this Town, and exhibited the Effigy of a certain Honourable Gentleman . . . and committed it to the Flames. The Reason assigned for the People's Dislike to that Gentleman, was, from being informed of his having several Times expressed himself much in Favor of the Stamp Duty."

This article tells about a Stamp Act protest. Nearly 500 people burned a dummy of a stamp collector in Wilmington, North Carolina.

The French and Indian War was fought over North American lands. Britain passed taxes on the colonies to help get back some of the money that had been spent on the war. Inset: This article appeared in the November 20, 1765, North-Carolina Gazette.

Britain Taxes the Colonies

From 1754 to 1763, Britain fought the French and Indian War over control of North America. Britain won the war, but it left the country owing money. Britain decided to raise money by taxing the colonies.

In 1765, Britain passed the Stamp Act, which taxed the colonists on all paper goods. North Carolinians were upset. They did not believe Britain had the right to tax them without their approval. In protest North Carolinians John Ashe and Cornelius Harnett formed a group of **patriots** called the Sons of Liberty. Some of the Sons of Liberty went to the stamp seller's home in Wilmington, North Carolina. They forced him to quit his job. By the 1770s, many North Carolinians began to think about independence.

Merchants made more money if they smuggled their goods so that they did not pay taxes on them. As in this painting, smugglers would slip their ships into a harbor at night to avoid getting caught. Inset: Penelope Barker held the Edenton Tea Party on October 25, 1774. After the Edenton Tea Party women began to boycott British goods, women throughout the colonies did the same.

North Carolina's Women Protest

Britain did away with the Stamp Act in 1766, but continued to tax the colonies on other products. These taxes led some colonists to **smuggle** the taxed goods. In 1773, Britain passed a law to try to stop smugglers. People in Boston, Massachusetts, protested by dumping a load of British tea into the ocean. Britain punished Boston by closing its harbor. North Carolinians sided with the Bostonians and sent food to help them.

Women in North Carolina protested by holding tea parties. In 1774, Penelope Barker from Edenton held a tea party. At the party the women promised that they would boycott British tea. That means they would not buy it. The women made tea out of sassafras roots and chicory instead. This was the first time in Colonial America that women took a **political** action against the government.

The First Continental Congress was held at Carpenter's Hall in Philadelphia, Pennsylvania. William Hooper, Joseph Hewes, and Richard Caswell represented North Carolina at Congress. Inset: The Mecklenburg Resolves were passed on May 20, 1775. It is said that after the resolves passed, the western part of North Carolina announced its independence from Britain.

North Carolina Prepares for War

In October 1774, William Hooper, Joseph Hewes, and Richard Caswell represented North Carolina at the First Continental Congress, in Philadelphia, Pennsylvania. They met with other Colonial leaders there and wrote a list of objections and sent it to Britain.

Britain did not answer Congress's list. Instead, in April 1775, Britain sent soldiers to Massachusetts. They fought the colony's patriots there in the first battle of the American Revolution.

North Carolina was prepared for revolution. People in western North Carolina had broken away from Britain on May 20, 1775. That same month patriots forced Josiah Martin, North Carolina's **loyalist** governor, to leave the colony. Then they formed their own government, called the North Carolina Provincial Congress. In June, Hooper, Hewes, and Caswell returned to Philadelphia for the Second Continental Congress.

This picture shows the Battle of Moore's Creek Bridge from the point of view of the North Carolinian patriots. They are fighting North Carolinian loyalists. This patriot win took place on February 27, 1776. Inset: William Hooper attended both of the continental congresses and also signed the Declaration of Independence.

North Carolina and the Revolution

The first Revolutionary battle in North Carolina was fought between its own colonists! In February 1776, the patriots beat the loyalists at Moore's Creek Bridge. It would be four years before another battle was fought in North Carolina.

In July 1776, the Continental Congress met to decide if they wanted to be independent of Britain. North Carolina told its representatives to vote for independence. A few months before the meeting, North Carolina's government had written the Halifax Resolves. In them the colony explained why it wanted freedom. North Carolina's representatives presented the resolves at the congress and pushed the colonies to vote for independence. On July 4, 1776, the colonies signed the **Declaration of Independence**. Then the colonies would have to fight to keep their freedom.

The Twelfth State

The last battle fought in North Carolina helped win the war. The battle was fought in March 1781. The British won the Battle of Guilford Courthouse, but they lost nearly three times as many men as the Americans did. This made it easier for the Americans to win at Yorktown, Virginia, in October 1781. This battle ended the fighting.

The war officially ended with the Treaty of Paris in 1783. The United States now needed a new government. In May 1787, the Constitutional Convention was held in Philadelphia to create a **constitution** for the nation. North Carolina's representatives to the convention would not sign the Constitution until a **Bill of Rights** was added. After the Bill of Rights was added, North Carolina signed the Constitution on November 21, 1789, and became the twelfth state.

Glossary

American Revolution (uh-MER-uh-ken reh-vuh-LOO-shun) Battles that soldiers from the colonies fought against Britain for freedom, from 1775 to 1783.

Bill of Rights (BIL UV RYTS) The part of the U.S. Constitution that explains the rights of citizens.

constitution (kon-stih-TOO-shun) The basic rules by which a country is governed.

Declaration of Independence (deh-kluh-RAY-shun UV in-duh-PEN-dints) An official announcement signed on July 4, 1776, in which American colonists stated they were free of British rule.

elected assembly (ih-LEK-ted uh-SEM-blee) A meeting with a lot of people who were chosen by their peers to attend.

inhabitants (in-HA-buh-tents) People who live in a certain place.

loyalist (LOY-uh-list) Having to do with people who sided with Britain during the American Revolution.

minutemen (MIH-net-men) Armed Americans who were ready to fight at a moment's notice.

patriots (PAY-tree-uts) American colonists who believed in separating from British rule.

persecuted (PER-sih-kyoot-ed) Treated badly because of race, religion, or political ideas.

pirate (PY-rut) Someone who attacks and robs ships.

political (puh-LIH-tih-kul) Having to do with the work of government or public affairs.

proprietors (pruh-PRY-uh-turz) People who were given a colony and who ran it.

protested (PROH-test-ed) Acted out in disagreement of something.

Quakers (KWAY-kurz) People who belong to a faith that believes in equality for all people, strong families and communities, and peace.

represented (reh-prih-ZENT-ed) Spoken for by others.

smuggle (SMUH-gul) To sneak something into the country.

23

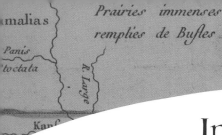

Index

Primary Sources

Page 4. *A Brief and true report of the New found land of Virginia in 1590.* map, The Mariners' Museum, Newport News, Virginia. **Page 6.** *Quakers Meeting.* Aquatint, 1809, Thomas Rowlandson and Augustus Charles Pugin after Joseph Constantine Baker, Bildarchiv Preussischer Kulturbesitz, Kunstbibliothek, Staatliche Museen zu Berlin, Germany. **Page 6. Inset.** Charter of Carolina. March 24, 1663, North Carolina State Archives, Raleigh, North Carolina. **Page 8. Inset.** Fundamental Constitutions of Carolina. March 1, 1669, North Carolina State Archives, Raleigh, North Carolina. **Page 10.** Men held captive in the Tuscarora War. Sketch, 18th century, Christoph von Graffenried, North Carolina State Archives, Raleigh, North Carolina. **Page 12. Inset.** George II. Oil on canvas painting, 1738, I. Whood. **Page 14. Inset.** *North-Carolina Gazette* article about a Stamp Act protest. November 20, 1765. **Page 16. Inset.** Penelope Barker. eighteenth century, John Wollaston, the Cupola House, Edenton, North Carolina. **Page 18. Inset.** *The Mecklinburg Declaration of Independence.* Medium, May 20, 1775, Rare Books and Special Collections Division, Library of Congress, Washington, D.C.

Web Sites